בס"ד

This book belongs to:

לד' הארץ ומלואה

Please read it to me!

Hachai

Way Too Much
Challah Dough

To Moshe, Sima, Shalom, Eliyahu, Chezky, Daniel, (and of course Otto) G.S.

• • •

In loving memory of my father, Boris. V.R.

• • •

First Edition - Elul 5766 / September 2006
Fourth Impression - Sivan 5770 / June 2010
Copyright © 2006 by HACHAI PUBLISHING
ALL RIGHTS RESERVED

Editor: Devorah Leah Rosenfeld
Managing Editor: Yossi Leverton
Layout: Unique Image Advertising

ISBN-13: 978-1-929628-23-0
ISBN-10: 1-929628-23-4

LCCN: 2005938157

HACHAI PUBLISHING
Brooklyn, New York
Tel: 718-633-0100 Fax: 718-633-0103
www.hachai.com info@hachai.com

Manufactured in Hong Kong, June 2010 by Paramount Printing

Glossary

Bubby	*Grandmother*
Challah(s)	*Traditional Shabbos loaf (loaves)*
Mitzvah	*One of the 613 commandments; good deed*
Shabbos	*Sabbath*

In honor of our beloved children
Fally, Blimi, Mendy, Yidy, Duvi, Chany,
Shmilly, Tziri, & Shaya

Avrum & Rivki Lemmer

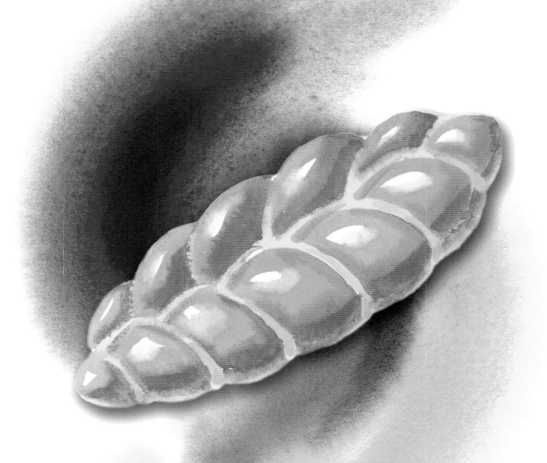

Way Too Much
CHALLAH DOUGH

by Goldie Shulman

illustrated by Vitaliy Romanenko

Hachai
PUBLISHING

**H**i there, I'm Mindy! Guess why I'm excited?
I'm baking challah – the first time I've tried it.

How do I start? What to mix? How to measure?
I called up my Bubby, who answered with pleasure.

"In a bowl of warm water, mix lots of fresh yeast
Add sugar and salt, half the flour at least
Put in oil and eggs, more flour, then – knead!
If you knead for ten minutes, you'll surely succeed.
Just follow each step and it doesn't take long.
Just follow directions and you won't go wrong!"

"Thanks, Bubby," I said, "That sounds really good!
I hope that my challah comes out as it should."

So I did what she said, and wouldn't you know,
In no time, I'd made a bowl full of dough.

Baking challah was fun – anybody could do it
I thought it was hard, but there's nothing much to it!

Just then, the phone rang, so what could I do?
My hands, full of dough, were as sticky as glue.
I washed them so quickly to get off that stuff.
I scrubbed and I rubbed… but not fast enough.

So back to the dough! It was still kind of lumpy.
The dough hadn't changed. It was sticky and bumpy.
I looked in the bowl and I started to doubt.
Had I done this correctly or left the yeast out?

Without yeast, a challah dough simply won't grow!
So I added some yeast right into the dough.

Right then, I heard ringing; the doorbell was chiming
Just look at my fingers – what terrible timing!
I knew it must be the delivery man.
When I got there, he'd already left in his van.

So, back to the dough! But then I forgot
Did I add all the yeast? Perhaps I had not!
Well that's easy to fix! We have plenty of yeast.
I guess it can't hurt if the yeast is increased.

Then I kneaded that dough just like Bubby had said.
'Till my shoulders were sore and my face was all red.

It was time for a break! I stared down at the dough,
And tried to tell if it had started to grow.
I watched as it lay in the bowl like a blob.
Maybe this yeast wasn't doing its job!

So I added some more of the yeast, just in case,
Hoping that this would help speed up the pace.

Would that dough ever rise? Well, I'd sure done my best.
Now I had to lie down for a ten-minute rest.
And while I was resting, and without my knowing,
The challah dough in that bowl just started growing!

The bowl I had picked for its very large size
Overflowed with fresh dough that continued to rise!
I took out a much bigger bowl for the dough
So it would have more than enough room to grow.

" Oh, no," I cried out, "It's reaching the top!"
I could see that the dough wasn't ready to stop.
I emptied the huge bowl right into the sink
"That's got to be just the right size, don't you think?"

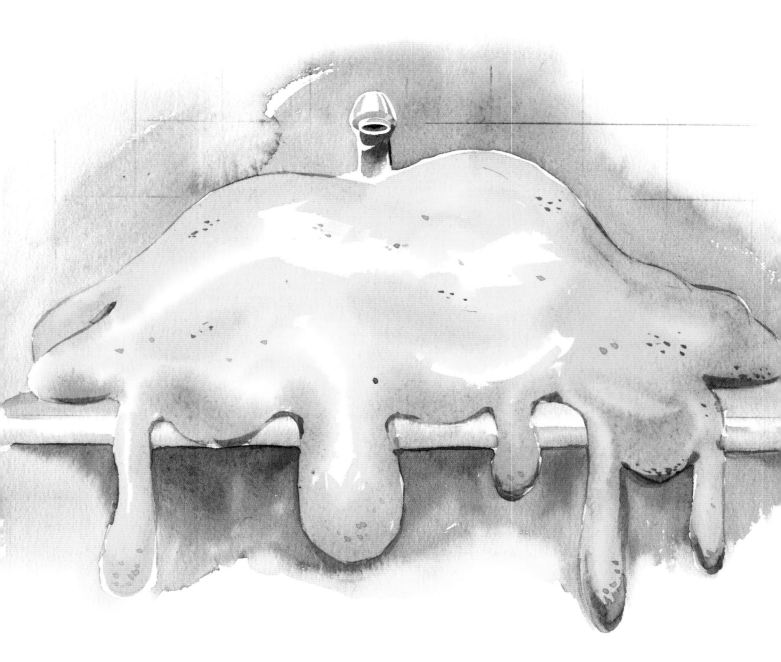

But that dough kept on rising, each second, each minute.
I must have put way too much extra yeast in it!
The sink was too small – I had no time to lose.
The toy box was bigger, so that's what I'd use!

I cleaned out the toys from the box in a wink,
And plopped in the dough that I'd dragged from the sink.

The toy box was big; it had plenty of space.
At last I had thought of the most perfect place!

But a few moments later, I saw I was wrong.
The dough was still growing; I didn't have long.

In shock, I sat down on a three-legged stool,
And that's when I spotted my old kiddie pool!
I tugged at the dough and I got it all in
But it rose even higher, right up to my chin!

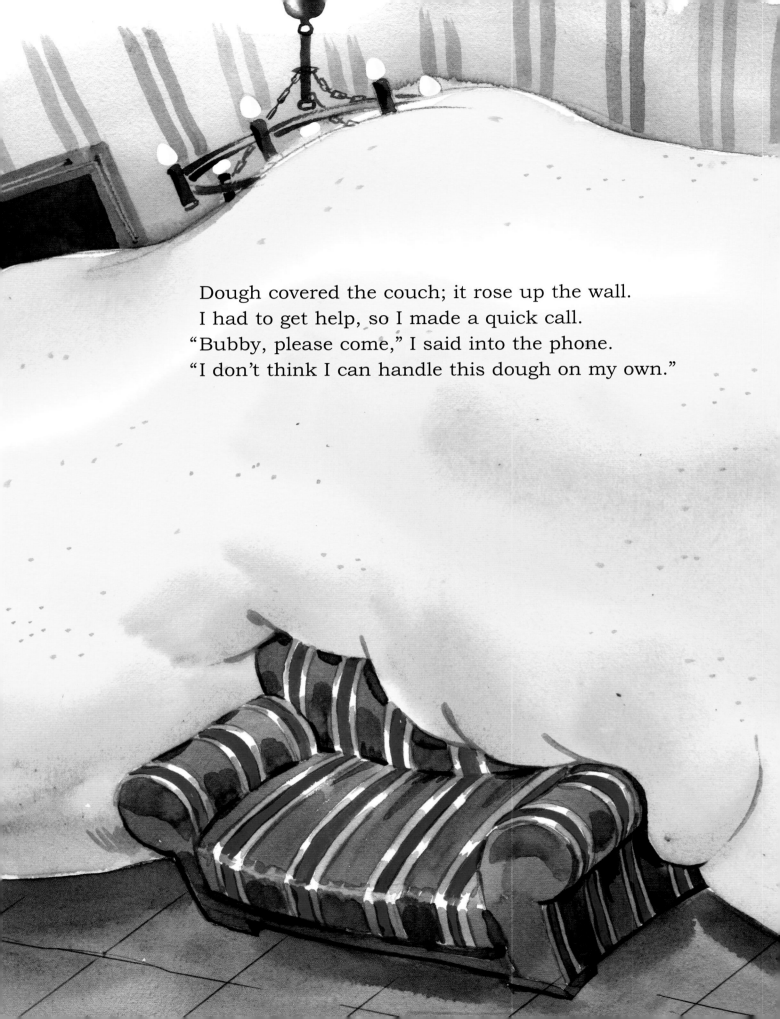

Dough covered the couch; it rose up the wall.
I had to get help, so I made a quick call.
"Bubby, please come," I said into the phone.
"I don't think I can handle this dough on my own."

Bubby came in three minutes; she looked all around.
Dough had oozed out the door, to the porch, to the ground!

"Did you follow directions?" "Oh, Bubby; I tried.
But I put too much yeast in my challah," I cried.

With her apron in place and a large metal tray,
Bubby walked toward the house and told me to stay.
How could she fix this? What would she do?
I wanted to go in the house with her, too.

But I followed directions and stayed in the yard
I wondered and waited and – boy! Was that hard!
As the seconds ticked by; all the dough cleared away,
And suddenly, Bubby appeared with her tray.

She held out two challahs, both perfectly braided
She looked at me calmly; her smile never faded.

"Baking challah," she said, "doesn't have to take long.
Just follow directions and you won't go wrong!"

I stretched out my hands; what a lovely surprise!
Then, all of a sudden, I opened my eyes...

The dough in my bowl had grown over the top,
That's as far as it got... just that far and it stopped.

My ten-minute nap had stretched on for an hour
I'd slept in my apron, all covered with flour.
It all felt so real; at least, that's how it seemed,
But the runaway dough was just something I dreamed.

I stood up and took "challah" out of my dough,
A small piece to burn – for the mitzvah, you know.

Bubby's coming for Shabbos, and proudly displayed
Will be my special challahs... completely home-made!

Bubby's Challah Recipe

INGREDIENTS:

4 ¾ or 5 cups warm water
(You can use up to 5 cups water if you use fewer eggs.)
3 Tbsp. dry yeast
(or one 2 oz. cake fresh yeast and 1 packet dry yeast)
1 - 1 ½ cups sugar

5 lb. bag of flour
3 - 5 eggs cracked and checked
(eggs with bloodspots must be discarded)
½ - ¾ cup oil
2 Tbsp. salt
1 egg, beaten
Sesame seeds (optional)

DIRECTIONS:

STEP 1: In a large, heavy-duty mixing bowl, add complete amount of water. Water should be warm to touch… not hot. Add yeast and sugar.   Allow to sit for 5-6 minutes.

STEP 2: Sift flour and pour 6 - 7 cups into the yeast mixture. Mix until it takes on a pasty look. Add 3 - 5 eggs. Then add oil and mix until smooth.

STEP 3: Take off 2 cups of the flour and put aside. Add whatever flour is left, and put in the 2 tablespoons of salt.

STEP 4: Time to knead the dough! For best results, knead with disposable gloves. Add small amounts from the 2 cups of flour you saved to add as you go. As soon as dough can be shaped into a ball, do not add any more flour. Remove the ball of dough from the bowl and transfer to a clean bowl to rise. Knead dough an additional 2 minutes in the clean bowl, adding a small amount of flour if dough is still sticky.

STEP 5: Rub 2 tablespoons oil on top of dough and cover with plastic wrap or a clean, damp dishtowel. Allow to rise for 2 hours, then punch down. Allow to rise another ½ hour.

STEP 6: Someone over bas mitzvah age now separates "Challah." See note below.

STEP 7: Shape Challah, place on greased loaf pans or cookie sheets, and allow to rise.

STEP 8: Preheat oven to 350°. Baste Challah with one beaten egg, using an egg brush, and sprinkle with sesame seeds. Place in oven. Check on small rolls after 20 minutes and on medium Challahs after 25 minutes. Can be baked until barely golden, or nicely browned, according to individual taste.

Yield: 5 medium Challahs and 12 small Challah rolls.

The Mitzvah of Separating Challah:

When preparing challah dough, it is a mitzvah to separate a small piece (approximately one ounce). For a recipe using this much flour, a brochah is then said:
"Boruch atoh…asher kidishonu b'mitzvosov vitzivonu l'hafrish challah,"
followed by the words: **"Harei zeh challah,"** and a private prayer if you wish.

In the days of the Beis HaMikdosh, the Holy Temple,
the separated portion would have been given to the Kohanim, the priestly tribe.
Nowadays, it is still not permitted for our personal use,
and is therefore kept apart from other foods and burned.

*Original recipe by Esther Blau, editor of The Spice and Spirit Cookbook.

Special thanks to Devorah Heller, the Challah Lady, for her simple one-bowl method.